JF MADDOX J

Maddox, Jake.

Playing forward /

PLAYING FORWARD

BY JAKE MADDOX

ILLUSTRATED BY SEAN TIFFANY

text by Eric Stevens

STONE ARCH BOOKS
a capstone imprint

Impact Books are published by Stone Arch Books
A Capstone Imprint
151 Good Counsel Drive, P.O. Box 669
Mankato, Minnesota 56002
www.capstonepub.com

Printe   sin.
0920
0056

Librar   e on the Library
of Co

Library Binding: 978-1-4342-1921-3
Paperback: 978-1-4342-2280-0

CREATIVE DIRECTOR: *Heather Kindseth*
ART DIRECTOR: *Kay Fraser*
GRAPHIC DESIGNER: *Hilary Wacholz*
PRODUCTION SPECIALIST: *Michelle Biedscheid*

TABLE OF CONTENTS

Team JAKE MADDOX

WILLY WILDCAT, COACH T, TREY, DANIEL, DWAYNE, ISAAC, PJ

#		Position	PPG	FT %	FG %	StI	
	Danny Powell	Center	9	73.2	82.8	5	
11	Daniel Friedland	Forward	5.7	95.8	85.1	12	
13	PJ Harris	Center	22	65.6	90.2	7	3
23	Trey Smith Ⓒ	Guard	14	96.2	80.5	20	8
26	Isaac Roth	Guard	11.5	94.1	79.3	11	
33	Dwayne Illy	Forward	6.2	82.9	77.9	9	1

Athlete Highlight: **Isaac Roth**

Isaac Roth is the 5'7 starting point guard for the Wildcats. He has the knowledge and attention it takes to lead his team to the win. He isn't a very high scorer, though.

ROTH
26
Center?
Guard?
26
Site
Leander
Wildcat Courts
Wildcat Courts
Cole Station
Wildcat Courts
Killeen
Killeen
Wildcat Courts
7:30
7:30
7:30
1:00

Chapter 1
ALL-STAR

Isaac Roth and his father sat on the edge of their seats. It was the first game for Westfield High School's basketball team. Isaac's older brother Eli was their forward.

Isaac watched his brother on the court. He was tall — six feet and three inches. When Eli got the ball, everyone watching knew they were in for a show. Eli was a great ball-handler, and had a great outside shot. In fact, he almost never missed.

But that's not why the fans cheered. Eli was at his best when he drove hard to the hoop.

It was already the fourth quarter. Westfield High was up by fifteen points, and everyone knew they'd win. Still, when the point guard passed to Eli, the place went crazy.

"Eli, Eli!" the crowd chanted. Isaac's brother faked a shot from the top of the key, then dribbled low past his defender, down the lane, and to the basket. He faked out the opposing center and leaped at the hoop. A hush fell over the crowd.

SLAM!

The crowd exploded with cheers as Eli's slam dunk hit home. Eli's size-thirteen sneakers hit the wood with a thud.

He smiled as he pumped his fist. Isaac and his dad jumped to their feet and cheered with everyone else.

"Hey, Dad," Isaac said over the roar of the crowd. "Look at that!" He pointed across the court at a small group of girls.

His dad squinted across the court. "Those girls?" he said. "What about them?"

"Wait a second," Isaac said. A moment later, as the girls jumped and cheered, they turned around and faced the crowd, screaming and shouting. Then Dad saw the backs of their shirts.

Each shirt had one word across the top of their backs, just like Eli's jersey: "ROTH."

Dad laughed. "Well, now I've seen everything," he said. "My son has his own cheerleaders."

Isaac laughed too. He didn't want to admit that he was jealous. He loved basketball too, and was even pretty good. But at only five feet and four inches tall, he couldn't make impressive shots and dunks like his brother could.

"Do you think I'll ever be as good as Eli?" he asked his dad.

"You're a great basketball player, Isaac," Dad replied.

"Thanks," Isaac said. "But I'm so short, especially compared to Eli. I'll never be able to do the things he does."

Dad put an arm around his younger son's shoulders. "You're only thirteen, Isaac," Dad said gently. "You'll get taller. After all, Eli wasn't always as tall as he is now."

Isaac didn't say anything, but he thought, *Yeah, but he was always way taller than me.*

Before long, the game was over. Eli had scored a total of 34 points, more than any other player. Total strangers were clapping him on the back and giving him high fives as he left the court. Isaac even saw the girls in the "ROTH" jerseys run over and give him hugs and kiss his cheek.

"Are we going to wait for Eli to get changed?" Isaac asked his dad.

"Of course," Dad said. "But let's wait outside where it's cool. It's hot in that gym."

The two of them leaned against their car to wait for Eli. The sun was down, and the night was a cool relief after the stuffy gymnasium.

"Tryouts are next week for the middle school team," Isaac said.

"Are you excited?" Dad asked.

Isaac shrugged. "Yeah, I guess," he said. "But I'm nervous, too."

"Ah, you'll make the team, no sweat," Dad said.

"But I want to start," Isaac said. "I want to be the starting power forward, like Eli."

"Well," Dad said, "I'm sure you'll make the starting five. Any position would be great, right?"

Isaac didn't say anything. Just then, Eli pushed through the heavy metal double doors on the side of the gym.

"Hey!" Eli called as he walked up.

"Great game, all-star," Dad said.

The three of them climbed into the car. Eli sat in the front, and Isaac got into the back seat.

"Isaac was just saying tryouts for the middle school team are next week," Dad said as they drove toward home.

"Oh yeah?" Eli said, looking back at Isaac. "Is Coach Turnbull still the man down there?"

"Yup," Isaac said, leaning forward. "He coached me last year, too. I didn't start last year, though. This year I hope I will."

"Oh, no doubt," Eli said. "You'll definitely make the starting five with your speed. I bet he'll make you point guard."

Isaac sighed. "I want to play power forward," he said. "That's where the points are. That's who everyone cheers for!"

Eli shrugged. "You've got the skills for point guard, little brother," he said. "Little guy, lots of speed, and you're sharp, too."

"'Little' is right," Isaac said under his breath.

"Besides," Eli added, "do you think no one ever cheered for Chris Paul, or Steve Nash, or John Stockton? Or Magic Johnson?"

Isaac sat back and slouched in the dark of the back seat. He leaned against the window and looked out at the white streetlights over the road as they whizzed past them.

I don't care about those guys. I want to play power forward, Isaac thought. *Like my big brother.*

Chapter 2
TRYOUTS

The tryouts were held the next Monday, right after the last class of the day. Isaac got changed into his shorts and last year's jersey in the locker room. Then he jogged out to the court.

"Hey, Isaac," PJ Harris said. PJ was the tallest member of the team. In fact, he was the tallest student at Westfield Middle School. If one player had the height to go pro one day, it was PJ.

"Ready for tryouts?" PJ asked. He held out his hand for a high five.

Isaac slapped his friend's hand. "Of course," he said. "I'm pretty sure I'll be starting this season. You will too. No doubt."

"Of course," PJ said. The two boys turned as the locker room door swung open and Dwayne Illy strode in.

"There's my competition," Isaac said.

"Are you hoping for power forward this season?" PJ asked. "Huh."

"What do you mean, 'huh'?" Isaac said.

PJ put his hands up and smiled. "Nothing, nothing," he said. "Dwayne is just really good at getting to the hoop. He's amazing from the foul line, too."

"I have a great free throw," Isaac said. "You know that. Better than yours!"

PJ laughed. "Man, my grandma's free throw is better than mine," he said.

Suddenly a whistle blew. PJ and Isaac turned and saw Coach Turnbull at the center of the court. All of the guys who were trying out gathered around him in a circle.

"All right, welcome to tryouts, everyone," Coach Turnbull said. "We're going to run drills and play a few short scrimmage games so I can get a good idea of what everyone can do out there."

Isaac glanced at Dwayne Illy. Dwayne was smiling. *He's so confident*, Isaac thought. He wished he felt as sure of himself as Dwayne did.

Coach T opened a big equipment bag at his feet and pulled out a bunch of red and yellow scrimmage jerseys. Each one was numbered.

"I'm going to call out numbers while you play," the coach said. "If I call your number, call back with your name so I know who you are. If you were on the team last year, I already know who you are."

Each of the players grabbed a jersey. Isaac and PJ both grabbed red jerseys. Dwayne picked up a yellow one.

Before the scrimmage, Coach Turnbull wanted the players to start with a layup drill. "Perfect," Isaac said to PJ as they lined up. "Dwayne's on the other team. This way I can show him up during the scrimmage. Steal off him, block his shots — really give him a hard time."

PJ shook his head. "You're fast, Isaac," he said. "And you know all of Coach T's plays better than anyone."

"What's your point?" Isaac asked. It was his turn to take a layup. He jogged up, caught his pass, and laid up the basketball. It went in off the backboard.

PJ jogged up next. "My point," he said as he shot his own layup, "is that you're a born point guard."

"Yeah, everyone keeps saying that," Isaac said. "But I don't want to play point guard."

After drills, Coach T called everyone to the middle to start the first scrimmage. Isaac and PJ were on a team with Trey Smith, a great shooter they both knew from seventh grade.

"Hey, Trey," Isaac said, calling him over.

Trey jogged over to PJ and Isaac. "What's up?" he said.

"You take the ball up, okay?" Isaac said.

Trey looked surprised. "Me?" he said. "You want me to play point?"

Isaac nodded, and Trey shrugged. "All right, I'll give it a shot," he said.

Isaac gave him a high five and the coach blew his whistle to start the scrimmage.

"No jump, Coach T?" PJ asked.

"Let's just say red ball to start," the coach said, smiling. "I think we all know PJ Harris would win a jump against anyone else in this gym."

Everyone laughed.

Isaac threw in to Trey to start play.

Isaac moved quickly down the court. He called out to Trey, "I'm open!"

Trey launched a pass to him, and Isaac barely got it. It was far off to the left. Isaac was able to spin through the yellow team's defense. He shot a quick layup.

"Yes!" he said as the ball fell in for two points.

"Nice recovery, Isaac," Coach T called out.

On defense, Isaac stayed close to Dwayne Illy. When a pass came to Dwayne on the yellow team's first play, Isaac managed to knock it out of bounds. Dwayne glared at him.

"What?" Isaac said, but Dwayne just turned away.

The next time up the court, Trey had trouble finding an open man. Isaac finally came to the top of the key and behind Trey.

"Give it here," Isaac said. Trey tossed him the ball, then moved toward the hoop. Isaac passed him the ball on one bounce. Trey shot and scored two points.

"Nice shot, Trey," the coach said. "And nice assist, Isaac. Way to take charge out there."

Isaac gritted his teeth. Coach T was already talking to him like he was a point guard.

This time on defense, Isaac was playing Dwayne even tighter. Dwayne caught a pass and tried to fake out Isaac, but Isaac wasn't fooled. He tapped the ball out of Dwayne's hands and grabbed it.

Then Isaac took off on a fast break.

"Great steal, Isaac!" PJ shouted, clapping.

Isaac reached the hoop and laid it up easily. Two more points.

PJ came jogging up the court. He gave Isaac a high five.

"I've got this in the bag," Isaac said. "Did you see me show up Dwayne? I'll be the next Wildcats forward for sure."

The whistle blew. "Okay, Isaac, take a seat for a little while," the coach said. "Let's see how these other boys do without you, okay?"

Isaac smiled and dropped onto the bench. *This is a cinch,* he thought. *I'll definitely be the starting power forward.*

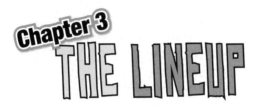

Chapter 3
THE LINEUP

"Hey, Isaac," PJ said. He stuck his head into the cafeteria and waved at Isaac. "You coming to Coach T's office? The starting lineup is posted."

Isaac popped a last tater tot into his mouth and nodded. "On my way," he said with his mouth full.

After he dropped his empty tray at the return counter, he jogged after PJ.

"The list has been up for at least ten minutes by now," PJ said. "We'll be the last two to check it, I bet."

Isaac shrugged as he jogged beside PJ toward Coach Turnbull's office. "I'm not worried," he said. "I already know what the list is going to say. Isaac Roth, starting power forward."

Just then, Dwayne Illy passed them, going the other direction. He looked at Isaac and smiled. "No hard feelings, Isaac," Dwayne said, and jogged on.

"What was that all about?" PJ asked.

"He was just being a good loser, I guess," Isaac said, "since he didn't get starting power forward. After tryouts on Monday there's no way the coach chose someone else over me."

PJ and Isaac rounded the corner. Then they stopped in front of the office door that read "Athletics Department." The team lineup was posted on the corkboard.

PJ leaned down to look at the list. "Uh-oh," he said.

"What?" Isaac asked, pushing PJ out of the way. "Didn't you make the team?"

"Sure," PJ said. "Starting center."

"So why the uh-oh?" Isaac asked. Then he saw it. "Starting power forward, Dwayne Illy," he said slowly.

Isaac looked at PJ. PJ nodded. "I guess you're our new point guard," PJ said.

Isaac curled his hands into fists. "I can't believe this!" he said. "What was Coach T thinking?" Then he pounded on the office door.

"Come in," the coach called. Isaac pushed the door open.

"Coach T, how could you make Dwayne power forward?" Isaac asked. "I played way better than he did yesterday."

"Yes, you did," the coach said. "But you'll do more for the team at point guard."

"More for the team?" Isaac said. "Point guards hardly ever score!"

"No, they assist," the coach said.

"But what about all my steals," Isaac said, "and doing better than Dwayne so many times at tryouts?"

"Dwayne Illy is a great power forward," Coach T said. "You're a great point guard, and that's final."

"But I don't want to play point guard," Isaac said.

"Well, you don't have to be on the team, of course," the coach said. He got up to lead Isaac out of his office.

"That's it, huh?" Isaac asked angrily.

The coach nodded. "If you want to be in the starting five, you're our point guard," he said.

Isaac stepped into the hall. Coach T closed the door behind him.

"Where's Dwayne?" Isaac asked.

PJ looked at him. "Um, eating lunch, I think," he said. "Why?"

Isaac took off like a shot. He was a fast runner. Seconds later, he was heading into the cafeteria.

He found Dwayne sitting at a big table by the window. Isaac stepped right up to him.

"Dwayne, you know you don't deserve to have power forward instead of me," Isaac said.

Dwayne just looked at him and frowned.

Isaac lightly pushed Dwayne's shoulder. "Well?" Isaac said. "Aren't you going to say anything?"

Dwayne just shook his head and went back to eating his hamburger.

Isaac grunted in frustration. Then he turned and headed for the door.

Chapter 4
FIRST PRACTICE

The team's first practice was that afternoon. Isaac didn't want to go.

"What's the point?" he asked PJ as they walked toward the locker room. "Coach T said I shouldn't bother coming if I won't play point guard."

"Right, but he meant that he wants you to show up," PJ said. "He wants you to play point guard."

"Yeah, I know," Isaac said, sighing.

The two boys got changed for practice and headed into the gym. Most of the team was already shooting around. After a few minutes, Coach Turnbull blew his whistle.

"Let's just start easy for our first practice, guys," the coach said. "Everybody, line up for layup drills."

He blew his whistle again. All of the players got into two lines for layups.

When it was Isaac's turn, he slowly jogged to the basket and tossed the ball up. It went in, but barely.

The coach said, "We're taking it easy, but show a little hustle out there, okay, Isaac?"

Isaac laughed. "It went in, didn't it?" he said. Then he went to the back of the rebound line.

"Watch the bad attitude, Isaac," the coach replied, frowning.

After drills, the boys split up into red and yellow teams for a scrimmage, just like they had during tryouts. Isaac and Dwayne Illy ended up on the red team together.

"Great," Isaac said sarcastically. "This will be really fun. I have to play on a team with the guy who stole my position."

PJ won the tip-off for the yellow team, and they scored two points right away. The red team brought the ball up the court. Isaac dribbled at the top of the key, looking for an open man to pass to.

Dwayne cut across the key and Isaac tossed him the ball. But it flew past Dwayne, landing a couple of steps behind him.

"Yellow ball," the coach said as the ball went out of bounds.

"Oh, well," Isaac said with a shrug.

Dwayne glared at him. "What?" Isaac asked. Dwayne just shook his head.

The next time Isaac was at the top of the key, the yellow team was up 4-0.

Dwayne got open again, and Isaac passed him the basketball. It flew at Dwayne like a bullet, this time a few steps ahead of him. Dwayne couldn't get to the pass in time.

PJ caught the pass instead. He threw it up the court at Trey Smith for the fast break. Now it was 6-0.

"You're going to lose the game for us," Dwayne said quietly to Isaac. "Unless you start playing like you care."

"Me?" Isaac shouted back. Everyone turned around. "Both of those failed drives were your fault!"

The coach jogged over and got between the boys. "What's the problem here?" Coach Turnbull asked.

"Dwayne is," Isaac said. "He missed both of my perfect passes, and he's blaming me because we're losing."

"Perfect passes?" Dwayne said. "Man, you must be crazy."

"Dwayne," the coach said, "go and have a seat on the bench for a minute."

"Me?" Dwayne said, looking surprised.

The coach nodded and Dwayne walked toward the bench.

"Isaac," the coach said, looking at him. "You played better in tryouts."

"Are you kidding? You're blaming me?" Isaac snapped. "First Dwayne was moving too fast and my pass went behind him. Then he was going way too slow, so my pass went in front of him. That guy can't play!"

"This isn't about blame," the coach replied. "This is about you. You haven't made an effort since we started drills an hour ago. Don't let your feelings about playing point guard affect your game, or you won't be on the team for long. Is that clear?"

"Oh, come on, Coach," Isaac said.

"Is it clear?" the coach asked again.

Isaac nodded. Coach Turnbull walked away and blew his whistle, then shouted to everyone, "Let's play ball."

Chapter 5
FIRST GAME

The first game of the season was at the end of the week. PJ and Isaac sat on the bench in the Wildcats locker room, tying up their sneakers.

"Are you still mad?" PJ asked.

Isaac sighed. "To be honest," he said, "yes."

"You need to get over it before Coach T kicks you off the team for good," PJ said. He stood up and bounced on his toes.

"I can shoot and dribble circles around Dwayne," Isaac said. "And you know it."

PJ shook his head. "Whatever. Let's just play, okay?" he said.

The two boys headed out to the gym. The team gathered around the coach.

The starters stood, and everyone else sat on the team bench. Other students and parents sat in the bleachers. They cheered as the Westfield Middle School Wildcats took the court.

PJ won the tipoff for the Wildcats and got the ball to Isaac right away. Isaac brought the ball up to the key and called a play. Dwayne would have to get open.

Isaac dribbled well. He controlled the ball with his right hand, staying out of reach of his defender.

Dwayne didn't have much trouble getting open, either. Isaac spotted him and passed the ball.

Dwayne hurried, but he didn't get to the ball in time. It flew out of bounds off a defender's fingers.

"Still Westfield ball," the referee called out.

"Nice catch, Dwayne," Isaac said with a laugh, rolling his eyes.

"Oh, you think it's my fault?" Dwayne said angrily.

The coach called over to Dwayne, "Keep your eyes open out there, Dwayne! That was a good pass."

Isaac smiled smugly at Dwayne, but he could see that Dwayne was mad.

After the throw in, Isaac took the ball to the top of the key and called the play again. He glanced up at the basket.

I should just get the two points myself, he thought. *Dwayne can't catch a pass anyway.*

Dwayne darted across the lane, and he got open for a few moments here and there. Isaac could have passed to him, but he didn't. Instead, he faked a jump shot, drove down the lane, and went for the layup.

But just as his foot left the ground, he got blocked by a defender who was nearly as tall as PJ. Isaac ended up on his butt in the paint.

"Time out!" Coach Turnbull called. He strode out to where Isaac sat on the court. The coach leaned over and gave Isaac his hand to help him up.

"Are you all right?" the coach asked as Isaac got up.

"Yeah," Isaac said with a nod.

"Good," the coach said. "I'm not happy," he added. Isaac looked at the coach's face. It was beet red. "If you pull another stunt like that," Coach Turnbull went on, "you're off the team. Dwayne was open five times, and you know it."

"What?" Isaac said, shocked.

"You heard me," the coach replied. He turned to the ref and nodded, then walked back to the Wildcats bench.

The referee blew his whistle. "Let's go," he said. "Visitor ball."

Isaac stomped his foot once, then fell back on defense. It was going to be a long game.

Chapter 6
A DEAL

The next day, Isaac left lunch a few minutes early and headed down the hall toward the athletics department.

Coach Turnbull's office door stood open. Isaac stuck his head inside. "Hey, Coach," he said.

"Come on in, Isaac," the coach said. He put down the papers he'd been looking at. "What's happening?"

Isaac sat down across from Coach Turnbull. "I want to make a deal with you," he said.

"What kind of deal?" the coach asked.

"Let me try playing power forward," Isaac said.

"Isaac, we've been over this," the coach said.

"Let me finish," Isaac said. "I'm just talking about one practice. One scrimmage."

"That's it?" the coach asked.

Isaac nodded. "That's it," he said. "If I can show you I'm better than Dwayne Illy, you'll move me to that position permanently."

"I don't know," Coach Turnbull said.

"And," Isaac went on, "if I am really better at point guard, I'll drop the issue forever and play point guard like you want."

The coach narrowed his eyes and stared at Isaac. "Hmm," he said.

"Is it a deal?" Isaac asked.

The coach stood up and nodded, then put out his hand. "Deal," he said.

Isaac smiled and shook the coach's hand. "All right!" he said. "Thanks, Coach."

"Now get to class," Coach Turnbull said, sitting back down.

Finally, Isaac thought as he jogged to his next class. *I'll prove to everyone that I belong at power forward.*

Chapter 7
SOMETHING NEW

"Listen up, everyone," Coach Turnbull said that afternoon in practice. "We're going to try some new positions today."

The other guys on the team whispered and looked around. Isaac snuck a glance at Dwayne, who was frowning.

PJ's eyebrows went up and he glanced at Isaac. "What is this?" he whispered, but Isaac just smiled.

"Dwayne Illy, I want you at point guard today," the coach said. "And Isaac Roth will be playing power forward. They'll be leading the yellow team. Everyone else, grab a jersey and let's get a five-on-five scrimmage started."

No one said anything, but Isaac could tell that the other players were surprised.

The yellow team got the ball first. Dwayne dribbled well and stood at the top of the key to call a play. Then he called the first play.

Isaac knew all the plays perfectly, since he normally called them. The play that Dwayne called meant the power forward would fall back for a sneak pass, and then drive up for a layup. Isaac headed back toward Dwayne, but just then Dwayne passed to PJ at the baseline.

PJ managed to catch the pass and tried to lay it up, but he was under the backboard. The ball bounced off the bottom and went out of bounds.

The coach blew his whistle. "Wrong play, Dwayne," he said. "You called for Isaac to come back, then passed to PJ. No one was ready for it."

"Sorry, Coach," Dwayne said. "I'm not used to playing point guard."

"All right, play ball," the coach said. He tossed the ball in to the red team.

On the yellow team's next drive, Dwayne took his time at the top of the key. He called a play for Trey Smith, but when Trey got open, Dwayne didn't pass him the ball.

"Trey is open!" Isaac called out.

Dwayne struggled at the top of the key, and then passed to Isaac.

Isaac tried to drive. He managed to lose a defender, but two other red team players swarmed over him. One of them stole the ball and threw it down the court for an easy fast break.

"You called for Trey and didn't pass to him," Isaac said. "He was wide open."

"I meant to call you up," Dwayne said. "Sorry. This is all new to me."

Isaac sighed. "It's cool," he said.

The next drive, Dwayne called the right play and passed to Isaac. Isaac drove hard to the basket. He thought about how his brother would do it, with a few spins and a slam dunk. Isaac couldn't dunk, but he had some dribbling skills.

He lost both defenders and put up a layup, but a strong arm fell over him and knocked him to the wood.

The coach blew his whistle. "Foul," he said. "Take two, Isaac."

Isaac went to the line. He almost never took foul shots, but he had a good outside shot. He looked at the rim, raised the ball, and shot.

Swish!

"Nice one, Isaac," the coach said.

On the next shot, the other players lining the lane got ready for the rebound. Isaac shot, but this time the ball fell to the right. PJ got the rebound and laid it up for two more.

"Good one, PJ!" Dwayne said.

When the red team was winning 18-8, the yellow team brought the ball up again. Dwayne called a play. Isaac had to cut across the lane, then right back, losing his defender. Dwayne would pass to him right in the middle of the lane, and Isaac should have an easy layup.

But Dwayne had the play backward. When Isaac cut across, Dwayne threw a pass like a rocket, but Isaac was facing the wrong way. The ball hit Isaac right in the back of the head, and he fell to the floor like a sack of bricks.

Chapter 8
BORN TO PLAY

Isaac got to his feet. He charged toward Dwayne. Someone yelled, "Fight!" But before Isaac could tackle Dwayne, Coach Turnbull pulled him away.

"No fighting!" the coach said.

"He beamed me in the head!" Isaac shouted, staring at Dwayne.

"It was an accident," Dwayne said. "I had the play backward. I'm used to seeing it from the other side, that's all."

"Oh, please," Isaac said. "You did it on purpose."

"It was an accident," the coach said.

"No way," Isaac said. He crossed his arms and looked at his sneakers. "He's blowing it, Coach."

The coach laughed. "He sure is," he said. "That's the point, Isaac. Dwayne isn't a general out there. He isn't usually keeping track of everyone's job and everyone's position."

Dwayne sat down on the bench and wiped his head with a towel. Isaac watched him catch his breath.

"You see, Isaac," the coach went on, "Dwayne's head is on his defender, and thinking about how to get another two points in that basket."

"So he's not a point guard," Isaac said.

"No, you are," Coach Turnbull said gently. "Your head is on everything at every moment. So yeah, you're small, and you can't weave through defenders as well as Dwayne. But you're doing something really important. You're leading the team on the court."

Isaac thought about it. It wasn't about being worse or better than Dwayne. It was about being right for point guard. "I get it, Coach," he said. Suddenly, instead of feeling small, he felt proud.

"All right then," the coach said. He turned to the bench. "Dwayne, come on in at power forward."

Dwayne smiled and jumped to his feet. He jogged out to the court.

"Play ball," the coach said. "Maybe we'll finally see some good plays today!"

The team laughed and the scrimmage began again. The yellow team brought the ball up. Isaac held it at the top of the key and called Dwayne across the lane. They connected perfectly.

Dwayne caught the pass and spun to his left, then back to his right. He easily shook his defender and went to the hoop.

Two points!

"Nice moves, Dwayne," Isaac said.

Dwayne laughed and said, "Nice pass, Isaac."

Isaac passed to Dwayne over and over. The two scored fourteen points for the yellow team.

Just before five o'clock, Isaac looked up and saw his father and brother sitting in the bleachers. They were a little early to pick him up from practice. Isaac waved, and his brother waved back.

The red team took the ball up. Their forward drove to the hoop, but PJ stopped him with a perfect block. The ball rebounded right to Isaac.

Isaac spun and signaled to Dwayne to get down the court quickly. Dwayne took off like a shot, and Isaac passed the ball just ahead of him. It was a perfect pass. Dwayne caught it and, after one dribble, easily laid it up for another two points.

"Great play, guys," the coach said. He blew his whistle. "That's it for today. I think we finally have a real point guard. Good job, Isaac."

Isaac smiled. He went over to his brother and father.

"When did you two get here?" Isaac asked.

"A while ago," his father said. "We missed your first game, so we wanted to see you in action."

Dwayne walked up. "This is Dwayne Illy," Isaac said. "He's our power forward."

"You two are some team," Isaac's dad said.

"Great assists, little brother," Eli said. "I didn't know you were so good. Point guard is a tough position."

"Nah," Isaac said. "Like you said, I have the right skills for it."

Isaac glanced at Dwayne. "Isn't that right, Dwayne?" he said.

"Oh, for sure," Dwayne replied.

"It would be ridiculous," Isaac added, "for me to play any other position."

"Yeah," Dwayne said. "It would be like if I played point guard."

"We better not ever let that happen," Isaac said. Dwayne and Isaac high-fived and laughed as they headed out to the parking lot.

THE AUTHOR
ERIC STEVENS

15

ERIC STEVENS LIVES IN ST. PAUL, MINNESOTA WITH HIS WIFE, DOG, AND SON. HE IS STUDYING TO BECOME A TEACHER. SOME OF HIS FAVORITE THINGS INCLUDE PIZZA AND VIDEO GAMES. SOME OF HIS LEAST FAVORITE THINGS INCLUDE OLIVES AND SHOVELING SNOW.

24

THE ILLUSTRATOR
SEAN TIFFANY

WHEN SEAN TIFFANY WAS GROWING UP, HE LIVED ON A SMALL ISLAND OFF THE COAST OF MAINE. EVERY DAY UNTIL HE GRADUATED FROM HIGH SCHOOL, HE HAD TO TAKE A BOAT TO GET TO SCHOOL! SEAN HAS A PET CACTUS NAMED JIM.

GLOSSARY

attitude (AT-i-tood)—how you feel about something

cinch (SINCH)—easy

defender (di-FEN-dur)—someone who is protecting something

doubt (DOUT)—uncertainty

frustration (fruhss-TRAY-shuhn)—a feeling of helplessness or discouragement

impressive (im-PRESS-iv)—effective, cool, or well-done

jealous (JEL-uhss)—wanting what someone else has

opposing (uh-POZE-ing)—on the other team

permanently (PUR-muh-nuhnt-lee)—for a long time

scrimmage (SKRIM-ij)—a game played for practice

DISCUSSION QUESTIONS

1. Isaac wants to be a power forward like his brother. Why is he upset when he is asked to play point guard?

2. Isaac makes a deal with the coach. What else could he have done if he was upset with his position?

3. How would you feel if you were given a position or role you weren't happy with? Talk about it.

WRITING PROMPTS

1. Try writing the first chapter from Eli's point of view. How does he feel during his game and the ride home?

2. Do you have any siblings? Write about your siblings.

3. Isaac is disappointed with his position. Write about a time you were disappointed.

MORE ABOUT POINT GUARDS

In this book, Isaac Roth is the point guard for the Westfield Wildcats. Check out these quick facts about point guards.

* Point guards are usually not as tall as other players on a basketball team. Height isn't as important for this position as it may be for other positions.

* A point guard's job is to be in control of the ball and make sure that the offense is being played correctly. He or she needs to pay attention to everything that's going on during a game.

* A point guard should have a good jump shot to be a well-rounded player.

* Famous point guards have included Chris Paul, Oscar Robertson, Magic Johnson, Steve Nash, Jason Kidd, Walt Frazier, Gary Payton, and John Stockton.